LEVEL 2 READER

POKÉMON™

Adventure on the Horizon

Adapted by Maria S. Barbo

©2024 Pokémon. ©1997–2023 Nintendo, Creatures, GAME FREAK, TV Tokyo, ShoPro, JR Kikaku. TM, ® Nintendo.

ISBN 978-1-5461-0983-9

10 9 8 7 6 5 4 3 2 1   24 25 26 27 28

Printed in the U.S.A. 40

First printing 2024

Designed by Cheung Tai

SCHOLASTIC INC.

Liko squirmed in her seat.
It was her first day of school.
And she was about to get her very first Pokémon!

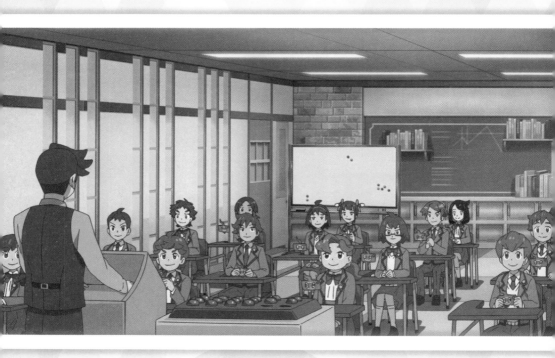

Liko slowly walked to the front of the room.
Her heart was racing.
I wonder who mine will be, Liko thought.
I hope we bond!

She chose a Poké Ball.
Sprigatito popped out!
"The Grass Cat Pokémon," her Pokédex said.
"It lets out a sweet scent with every step!"

"You're the cutest!" Liko squealed.
She reached out to hug her new partner.
"Reow!" Sprigatito scratched her and ran away.

Why? Why? Why? Liko thought.
I'm SO not ready for this!
She chased Sprigatito, and soon saw it was way up on the roof.

"Sprigatito!" Liko called.
"It's dangerous up there!"
The Grass-type Pokémon
shrugged.
It walked over to the edge.
Then it leaped off toward Liko!

"Please don't jump down!" Liko cried.
Fwump! Sprigatito landed on Liko's face.

Liko lost her balance.
They both tumbled over the railing!
"Waaaaaah!" Liko screamed.

Boing!

Liko and Sprigatito bounced off a Snorlax's belly and landed safely on the grass.

"That was a close one!" Liko said.
She turned to her Pokémon.
But Sprigatito was already gone.
"Sprigatito!" Liko cried. "We're supposed to
have a bond!"

Liko didn't understand what she was doing wrong.

Her Pokémon partner kept running away!

She followed Sprigatito's sweet scent to the lake.

"You're here! Thank goodness!" Liko said.
She tried for another hug.
Bop! Sprigatito whacked her in the eye.
"Ah! Why though?!" Liko howled.

Their first Pokémon battle wasn't much better.
"Okay, Sprigatito," Liko said. "Use—"
But Sprigatito didn't listen.
It sprang at Oshawott with its claws out.

Whoosh!

Oshawott blasted Sprigatito with its Water Gun move.

Sprigatito crash-landed at Liko's feet.

"Well, you won't become a champion like that," said Oshawott's Trainer.

Sprigatito was always doing its own thing.
It napped instead of training.
It hated to snuggle.
And it never listened.

Liko decided to study her Pokémon.
She made a map of Sprigatito's nap spots.
And lots of lists.
She even set up secret training sessions!

But Sprigatito seemed bored.
"Sprigatito, use Leafage!" Liko called.
Her Pokémon just yawned.

"Use Leafage!" she tried again.

Sprigatito glowed green for a second, then stopped.

Why can't we bond? Liko wondered.

After training, Liko couldn't sleep.
She took out her favorite necklace.
Her grandma had given it to her.

She'd said it would protect Liko.

"I wish it could help me bond with Sprigatito," Liko groaned.

The next day, a stranger came to the school.
He told Liko her grandma had sent him.
"She wants you to come with me," he said.
"And bring the necklace."

Sprigatito hissed.
Liko knew something wasn't right!
They ran back to their room.
Liko put on her necklace and escaped out the window.

The stranger followed them!
He threw out a Poké Ball.
"Now, Rhydon!" he called.
Sprigatito leaped in front of Liko.
It *wanted* to battle this time!

"I guess we're doing this!" Liko said. "Use Leafage!"

The stranger laughed at her.

"You can't beat Rhydon with that move."

But Liko knew they didn't have to beat Rhydon.
Sprigatito's swirl of leaves went in
Rhydon's eyes.
Rhydon couldn't see them!
The partners ran away.
"That was SO cool!" Liko cheered. "We actually used a move together!"

The stranger chased them up to the clock tower.

"I won't hurt you! Just give me the necklace!" he shouted.

"Yeah, right!" Liko said. "Like I believe that!"

The man threw out another Poké Ball.
"Ceruledge, use Bitter Blade!" he called.
"Stay back!" a new voice shouted.
A man swooped down on a Charizard.

"What is happening right now?" Liko wondered.

Charizard and Ceruledge began to battle.

"We have to get out of here!" Liko told Sprigatito.

"Reow!"

Sprigatito and Liko ran to the edge of the roof.
Together, they jumped off.

Liko's necklace glowed.
It hugged them in a ball of light.
It was protecting them!
Just like her grandma said it would.

Liko hugged Sprigatito.
They had finally bonded.
"I had to take a leap," Liko said.
"This is the start of something big!"